Mr. Posey's New Glasses

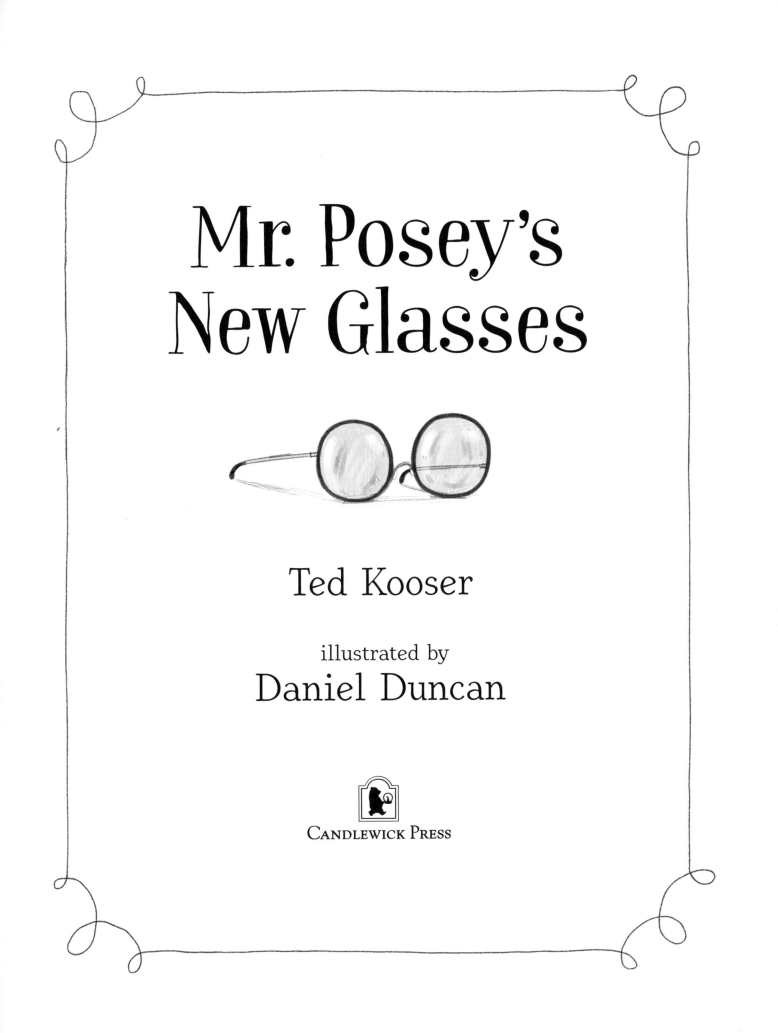

Ted Kooser

illustrated by
Daniel Duncan

CANDLEWICK PRESS

M r. Posey was tired of his old eyeglasses.
When he put them on, everything looked
dull and boring.

There sat his table, under the same old kitchen window, and on it sat his same old cup and spoon and newspaper.

When he bent over the paper to read it, nothing in it was new. On the front was the same old picture of the mayor, shaking the same old somebody's hand. On the sports page, there was the same high-school track star dashing across the finish line with his arms in the air.

Even the picture of the beef roast in the grocery store advertisement looked like it was the same old roast that it had always been.

No matter where he looked, everything seemed blurred and dull.

Beyond his window was his same old backyard, and beyond the hedge was Mrs. Bloomer's same old laundry drying on her same old clothesline.

Mr. Posey's friend Andy was throwing a stick for Mrs. Bloomer's dog, Parker, and Parker was barking at Andy. To Andy and Parker, nothing was ever dull; every day was interesting.

But no matter where Mr. Posey looked, everything was the same as it had been FOREVER. He wanted to look at the world with excitement, to see it the way Andy saw it. Today might be just the day to get new glasses. New glasses might fix everything!

And since Andy was always looking for something new to do, Mr. Posey went outside and called across the hedge, "Andy, want to help me buy new glasses?"

"Sure!" said Andy, and he dropped the stick. "Can Parker come along?"

"Well, I guess so," said Mr. Posey.

Mr. Posey bought all his clothes at the Cheer Up Thrift Shop. He bought his same old shoes; he bought his same old socks. All the shirts he bought looked just the same because they were the same, exactly. When he opened the door, the same little bell jingled once to alert the clerk, the same skinny man who was always going through cardboard boxes at the back of the shop, that he had a customer.

The shop smelled the same as it always smelled, like rose petals that somebody had kept in an old shoe. When Mr. Posey and Andy walked around, the floor creaked exactly the way it always creaked.

In the middle of the shop was a cardboard barrel full of glasses. Mr. Posey plunged his hand in and stirred the glasses around and fished out a pair that had big stars for frames, blue plastic stars, with imitation diamonds all along the temples.

He put his old glasses in his shirt pocket, where he always put them, and put on the new glasses, fitting the tips over his ears, and when he looked through the lenses, all he could see was . . .

a night sky. He saw the Big Dipper. He saw the Little Dipper. He saw Orion lying along the horizon. He saw a plane with one light blinking, so far above him that he couldn't hear the whoosh. A shooting star shot through the corner of one lens. Somewhere in the darkness, an owl was hoo-hoo-hooing very faintly.

These glasses are really new, thought Mr. Posey, *but they make the world much too dark. If I bought them, I wouldn't be able to see my cup on the table, or read my newspaper, or look out the window and see my friend Andy throwing a stick for Parker.*

So he took them off and put them back, but Andy pulled them out again and put them on. "Wow! Cool!" he said. "Instant midnight!"

Andy dropped the glasses in the barrel and pulled out a different pair. "How about these?" he asked, handing them to Mr. Posey. The plastic frames were stripy, brown and tan, and looked as if they had been cut from the shell of a turtle and then carefully polished. A pair of glasses like that would surely not be the same old thing, Mr. Posey thought, and so he tried them on. Andy watched with interest.

In an instant Mr. Posey felt cold and wet, as if he were in deep water, and he sucked in his breath and held it.

An enormous gray fish with big yellow eyes and a bent fishhook in its lower lip came slowly swimming toward him, looking very hungry. And in both lenses, he could see the shapes of other fish, even bigger than the first, now slowly turning and swimming in his direction. And then he saw a huge tentacle reaching toward him, its suckers opening and closing.

He snatched off the glasses and threw them back in the barrel, and all the fish and the tentacle vanished. Mr. Posey took a deep breath of the familiar Cheer Up Thrift Shop air, with its rose-petal old-shoe smell. He wouldn't try on those glasses again! Ever!

"Let me try those!" said Andy, and he picked them out of the barrel and put them on. "Wow!" he said. "This is like being a deep-sea diver, but you don't have to breathe through a tube! Let's see what else is in there."

Andy reached way down in the barrel and scrabbled
around and pulled out another pair—a pair with big,
perfectly round lenses—and handed them to Mr. Posey.
They looked safe enough, but when Mr. Posey put them on . . .

the world began to swirl, like water going down a drain.
The Cheer Up Thrift Shop, with its used shirts and housedresses
and pots and pans and books and pictures, whirled around him
faster and faster. And the clerk unpacking boxes sped past
him again and again.

Mr. Posey felt as if he was going to be sick, and to keep his balance, he held on to the rim of the cardboard barrel. Quickly he snatched off the glasses and handed them to Andy, who put them on and immediately began to get dizzy, too.

Andy flung the glasses back in the barrel. "Those are really awful!" Andy said. But everything was slowing to a stop, and the shop was pretty much the same as it had been before. Mr. Posey felt very much relieved and so did Andy, who wandered away to see what else he could find that might be fun.

Getting new glasses was becoming more and more scary, and Mr. Posey was already tired. He was starting to be afraid even to touch any of the glasses in the barrel. There was a bucket of rulers nearby; he picked one out, leaned over the barrel, and used the ruler to stir through the glasses.

Beneath the star glasses and the turtle-shell glasses and the perfectly round ones, Mr. Posey found a pair whose lenses were shaped like the eyes of a cat.

He carefully lifted them out with the ruler so as to
avoid touching any of the others, then put them on.

Suddenly he could hear dogs barking, not little dogs like Parker but big dogs with barks that came from deep inside their stomachs. And the barks were quickly turning into terrible growls and coming closer! Suddenly he could see dogs racing toward him from every direction, their fangs bared and dripping!

Quickly he snatched the glasses off and the barking died away and the dogs were gone. He was glad that Andy hadn't tried them on. But he wasn't ready to give up on finding new glasses. With the ruler, he fished out a pair of wire-rimmed glasses with lenses too scratched to see through . . .

and then he tried on a pair of reading glasses, but with them on, he couldn't do anything but read, and there were other things he wanted to see and do.

There was a pair with pink lenses that made everything pink, but who would want that?

Mr. Posey was getting discouraged. He put his old glasses on, sighed, and looked around.

Andy came walking up carrying something. "Could you buy this for me?" he asked Mr. Posey.

"I'd be happy to, Andy," he said, squinting through his old glasses, "but I can't quite see what you've got."

"It's no wonder," Andy said with a smile. "Your glasses are so dirty, it looks as if a dog like Parker has been licking them."

"Dirty?" said Mr. Posey.

"Filthy," said Andy. "Icky, yucky."

Mr. Posey pulled his handkerchief out of his pocket and wiped the lenses. Then he looked all around.

The racks of clothing looked the same, but the colors of the shirts and blouses were brighter. The bucket of rulers still looked like a bucket of rulers, but now they looked like something somebody would like to pick up and have fun with. Mr. Posey was greatly relieved. His old glasses were fine—they'd just been dirty! He took them off, wiped them again, and put them back on.

Then he looked at what Andy was holding: a wheel with pedals on either side, like one from a tricycle. "What do you want it for?"

"I don't know yet," said Andy, "but I'll think of something."

Together they walked to the front of the store, where the clerk was now waiting at the cash register.

"How much for the wheel?" Mr. Posey asked.

"How about a quarter?" said the clerk. "Do you need any new pants? I'll sell you a pair for another quarter!"

"No, but thank you anyway," said Mr. Posey. "I'll bet my old pants will look better now."

"Why's that?" asked the clerk.

"Oh, never mind," said Mr. Posey, smiling at Andy as Andy smiled back.

So Andy with his wheel and Mr. Posey with his clean glasses left the Cheer Up Thrift Shop and strolled toward home. Mr. Posey felt kind of bouncy—it felt really good to see things in a way he never had before. Now and then, they stopped and Mr. Posey slowly turned all the way around so he could see everything.

Though his street looked pretty much the same, it also looked just a little different, a little newer. The houses of his neighbors and their front yards with their rosebushes looked pretty much the same, but cleaner and neater. Andy was the same, too, but he looked happy to be carrying a wheel he'd never carried before. Now and then, he'd put it down and pedal it along using his hands.

And as they passed Mrs. Bloomer's house, Mr. Posey could see her same old laundry hanging in the side yard, and Parker started barking and barking. Even though these things looked the same, somehow the world seemed brighter than before; it was different and exciting.

To Henry Langmack
T. K.

First edition 2019

Library of Congress Catalog Card Number pending
ISBN 978-0-7636-9609-2

19 20 21 22 23 24 CCP 10 9 8 7 6 5 4 3 2 1

Printed in Shenzhen, Guangdong, China

This book was typeset in Youbee.
The illustrations were created digitally.

Candlewick Press
99 Dover Street
Somerville, Massachusetts 02144

visit us at www.candlewick.com